GREEN SEA TURTLE

A **NESTING** JOURNEY

REBECCA HIRSCH
AND MARIA KORAN

www.av2books.com

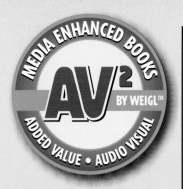

Go to **www.av2books.com**, and enter this book's unique code.

BOOK CODE

P 9 3 7 7 7 2

AV² by Weigl brings you media enhanced books that support active learning.

AV² provides enriched content that supplements and complements this book. Weigl's AV² books strive to create inspired learning and engage young minds in a total learning experience.

Your AV² Media Enhanced books come alive with...

Audio
Listen to sections of the book read aloud.

Key Words
Study vocabulary, and complete a matching word activity.

Video
Watch informative video clips.

Quizzes
Test your knowledge.

Embedded Weblinks
Gain additional information for research.

Slide Show
View images and captions, and prepare a presentation.

Try This!
Complete activities and hands-on experiments.

... and much, much more!

Published by AV² by Weigl
350 5ᵗʰ Avenue, 59ᵗʰ Floor
New York, NY 10118
Website: www.av2books.com

Library of Congress Cataloging-in-Publication Data

Names: Hirsch, Rebecca E., and Koran, Maria.
Title: Green sea turtles : a nesting journey / Rebecca Hirsch and Maria Koran.
Description: Minneapolis, MN : AV2 by Weigl, [2017] | Series: Nature's great journeys | Includes bibliographical references and index.
Identifiers: LCCN 2016004423 (print) | LCCN 2016011669 (ebook) | ISBN 9781489645173 (hard cover : alk. paper) | ISBN 9781489649928 (soft cover : alk. paper) | ISBN 9781489645180 (Multi-user ebk.)
Subjects: LCSH: Green turtle--Migration--Juvenile literature. | Green turtle--Juvenile literature. | Animal migration--Juvenile literature.
Classification: LCC QL666.C536 H557 2017 (print) | LCC QL666.C536 (ebook) | DDC 597.92/8--dc23
LC record available at http://lccn.loc.gov/2016004423

Printed in the United States of America in Brainerd, Minnesota
1 2 3 4 5 6 7 8 9 0   20 19 18 17 16

072016
071416

Project Coordinator: Maria Koran   Art Director: Terry Paulhus

Every reasonable effort has been made to trace ownership and to obtain permission to reprint copyright material. The publishers would be pleased to have any errors or omissions brought to their attention so that they may be corrected in subsequent printings.

Weigl acknowledges Getty Images, iStock, Dreamstime, Alamy, Minden, and Shutterstock as its primary image suppliers for this title.

Contents

GREEN SEA TURTLES

Green sea turtles spend their lives at sea. But they return to land for a short time every few years. They migrate many miles across the open ocean. The females return to land to lay their eggs. The males remain in the water by the shore. The eggs soon **hatch** and out crawl tiny turtles. They head for the water. The turtles swim far out to sea. They spend the first part of their lives in the open ocean. Then the young turtles join the adult turtles in underwater meadows near the shore.

The green sea turtle's lifetime journey is its migration. This is when an animal moves from one **habitat** to another. Migrations happen for many reasons. Some animals move to be in warmer weather where there is more food. There they can reproduce, or have their babies. And these migrations can be short distances, such as from a mountaintop to its valley. Or they can be long distances, like the green sea turtle's journey.

Green sea turtles live in the ocean.

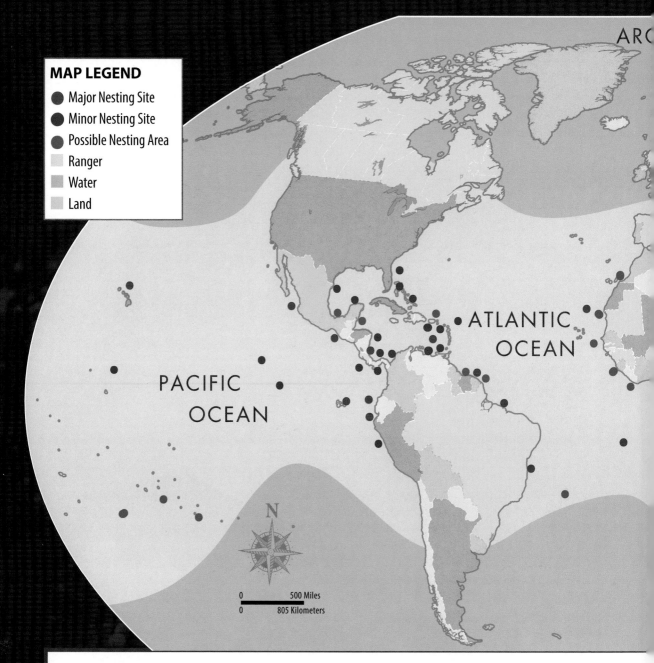

MAP LEGEND
- ● Major Nesting Site
- ● Minor Nesting Site
- ● Possible Nesting Area
- ▢ Ranger
- ▢ Water
- ▢ Land

ATLANTIC
OCEAN

PACIFIC
OCEAN

N

0   500 Miles
0   805 Kilometers

MIGRATION MAP

G reen sea turtles live in warm waters all over the world. They swim in the Atlantic, Pacific, and Indian oceans. They tend to live near land. They are found along coasts, around islands, and in bays. In the United States, green sea turtles are found near the Florida coast, at the southern tip of California, and near Hawaii.

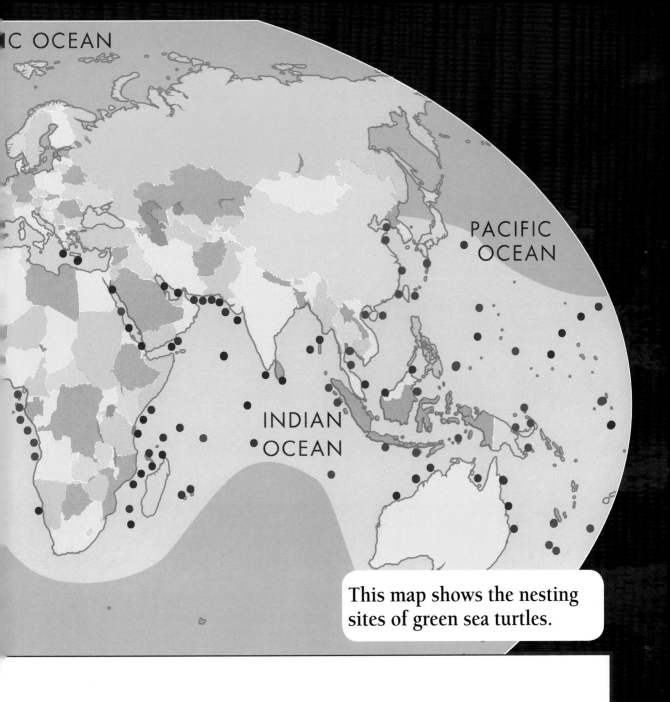

PACIFIC OCEAN

INDIAN OCEAN

This map shows the nesting sites of green sea turtles.

Adult green sea turtles leave the sea grass meadows every two to four years. Green sea turtles have a **reproductive** migration. They migrate across the ocean. They return to their **natal beaches**. That is where their eggs will hatch. The beaches are along the coasts of continents and in the Caribbean and Hawaiian Islands. Some green sea turtles may travel more than 2,600 miles (4,200 km) on their journey.

One of the largest turtles on Earth lived millions of years ago. It could grow to be 13 feet (4 m) long.

SEA TURTLES

Green sea turtles are just one kind of sea turtle. Other sea turtles are the leatherback, loggerhead, hawksbill, olive ridley, Kemp's ridley, and flatback.

Sea turtles are **reptiles**. They have scales, lay eggs, and are **cold–blooded**. This means the outside temperature changes their body temperatures. Sea turtles swim close to the water's surface to get warm. The green sea turtle even climbs onto shore to sit in the sun.

Green sea turtles grow to be very large. They can weigh as much as 420 pounds (190 kg). And they can grow to be 4 feet (1 m) long. The biggest green sea turtle ever found weighed 871 pounds (395 kg). That is the size of a large grizzly bear!

To warm themselves, green sea turtles sometimes come on land.

Green sea turtles do not look very green. The color of their top shells can be black, gray, green, yellow, or brown. The top shell is called a **carapace**. Their bottom shell is called a **plastron**. It is white or yellow. But underneath the shell, the turtle's fat is green. This is probably from the sea grass and algae the turtle eats. It is the color of its fat that gives the green sea turtle its name.

Long flippers make the green
sea turtle an excellent swimmer.

LIFE AT SEA

Green sea turtles are suited for life in the ocean. Their shells are light and their bodies have a smooth shape. The turtles easily swim through the water. They paddle their front limbs to swim. These limbs are shaped like flippers. They use their back flippers to move in the right direction. They can move through the water as fast as 35 mph (56 kmh).

Green sea turtles spend most of their lives in the ocean. But they still act like land animals. They have lungs and breathe air. Green sea turtles come to the water's surface every few minutes to breathe when they swim. When they sleep, green sea turtles can stay underwater for more than two hours. Young green sea turtles cannot stay underwater that long. They sleep floating on the water's surface.

Algae and sea grass are food for green sea turtles.

Green turtles cannot pull their head and legs inside their shells. they do not have teeth. Ridges on their sharp beaks help them cut through tough sea grasses.

After swimming many miles, green sea turtles reach their natal beaches.

TO THEIR NATAL BEACHES

Every few years, adult green sea turtles leave the waters where they live. They set off across the deep sea. The turtles swim for many days. They move through the water at fast speeds. They use their strong flippers to push through the ocean.

Green sea turtles cover hundreds or thousands of miles during their migration. They swim through the ocean at a speed of 1 to 1.5 mph (1.5 to 2.3 kmh). The turtles might swim 30 miles (48 km) in a day. They arrive at their nesting grounds after a month or more. Males swim near the shore and look for females to mate with. After they mate, the females crawl onto the beaches. The males stay behind in the water.

A female waits until night to go onto the beach. She drags herself along the beach with her front flippers. She finds a high spot on shore. There the tide will not wash her eggs away. Then the female digs her nest. She makes a pit with her front flippers.

Then she uses her back flippers. She scoops out a space for the eggs in the pit. Finally, she puts her body over the space. She lays her **clutch** inside. A clutch is usually more than 100 eggs. The eggs drop gently into the nest. Each egg is about the size of a ping-pong ball. She lays all her eggs. Then she covers the hole with sand. She carefully packs down the sand. She leaves no trace of the hole. Then she crawls back to the water.

The female will nest again and again in the next few weeks. She will lay three to four clutches. Then the female's work is done. She leaves the beach and swims back out to sea. She must return to her feeding grounds. She will not see or care for her young. The baby turtles will be on their own.

A HATCHLING'S LIFE

Back in the nest, the baby turtles grow in their eggs. The temperature of the sand is important. It is what makes the baby turtles male or female. In warm sand, more females will hatch. In cool sand, there will be more males.

The baby turtles are called **hatchlings**. They are ready to come out of their eggs after two months. The egg's shell is like leather. It does not break. Each hatchling tears out of its egg. The turtle uses an egg tooth. It is a spike on the turtle's nose. Working together, the 2-inch (5 cm) long hatchlings then dig out of their nests. They wait just under the sand until it is night. Then the black or brown hatchlings quickly crawl to the sea.

Each egg is about the size of a ping-pong ball.

Soon baby turtles hatch from the eggs.

The baby turtles often cannot see the ocean from their nest. But they know which way to crawl. How do they do it? The hatchlings watch the sky. At night, the sky is brighter over the ocean. Light bounces off the water's surface. The turtles follow the bright sky and move toward the ocean. They leave tiny trails behind them in the sand. They fling themselves into the water. And they swim out into the great sea.

The green sea turtle's first year is filled with danger. Raccoons and skunks dig the eggs from nests. **Predators** wait on the beach as the baby turtles crawl to the water. Raccoons and crabs snatch the hatchlings. Seabirds pick them from the sand and water. Sharks track the turtles as they swim out to sea. Only one or two turtles in each clutch will survive their first year.

Green sea turtles live for 50 to 80 years. Some may even live to be 100.

A hatchling crawls on the sand toward the sea.

After leaving the open sea, the turtles move to shallow water where sea grass grows.

JOINING THE ADULTS

The young turtles swim out into the open ocean. This is where they will live for several years. They swim on the surface and float on mats of seaweed. They eat a mix of plants and small animals such as worms, shrimp, and jellyfish. Scientists call this time in a green sea turtle's life the "lost years." No one knows much about what the turtle does in these years. It is difficult to study the turtles. They live far out at sea away from people.

After several years in the open ocean, the young turtles swim toward land. They join the adults in shallow waters near islands and off coasts where sea grass grows. This is where they will spend the rest of their lives. The underwater meadows are the perfect habitat for green sea turtles. There is plenty of food for the turtles to eat. There are predators here, too. Tiger sharks swim nearby. But the turtles are ready. They dive down if they see a tiger shark. They avoid being attacked from below.

Young turtles cannot mate for many years. Green sea turtles are able to mate when they are 20 to 50 years old. Then they begin migrating to their natal beaches.

AMAZING SENSES

Green sea turtles have an amazing sense of direction. Hatchlings in the ocean for the first time somehow know where to swim. They find their way to the open sea and their feeding grounds. Adult green sea turtles migrate from their feeding grounds to their natal beaches. The rough sea pushes and pulls the turtles. But they are able find their way without their parents to guide them.

How do green sea turtles find their way across the ocean? No one knows how they do it. They seem to be able to sense the earth's magnetic field. This is a force in the earth. It is what makes a compass needle point north. Migrating sea turtles have a kind of compass in their bodies. They can use the earth's magnetic field as a guide as they journey across the sea. Green sea turtles may also smell or taste their way to the natal beaches.

The box jellyfish has the most deadly sting in the world. But the poison does not hurt the green sea turtles. They eat the jellyfish and keep beaches safe for people.

GREEN SEA TURTLES IN TROUBLE

Sea turtles seemed to be everywhere hundreds of years ago. Christopher Columbus wrote of the many turtles he saw near the Caribbean Islands. Many green sea turtles swam near the Cayman Islands. So he named the island "Las Tortugas." It is Spanish for "The Turtles."

But today green sea turtles are in serious trouble. There were once millions of green sea turtles worldwide. Today there are fewer than 100,000 nesting females. Green sea turtles are **endangered** animals. The number of green sea turtles around the world may continue to fall. If so, green sea turtles could disappear forever.

One big problem for the turtles is that people catch and eat them. People scoop eggs out of the turtles' nests. They take adults off nesting beaches. And people catch turtles as they swim through their feeding grounds. In some places green sea turtles are hunted faster than they can have babies. That is one reason the number of green sea turtles has fallen.

Fishing lines and nets are another problem. Swimming turtles can become tangled in fishing lines and nets. Nets that drag on the bottom of the ocean cause great harm. Green sea turtles get trapped in these nets. They drown because they cannot breathe underwater.

Today green sea turtles are endangered animals.

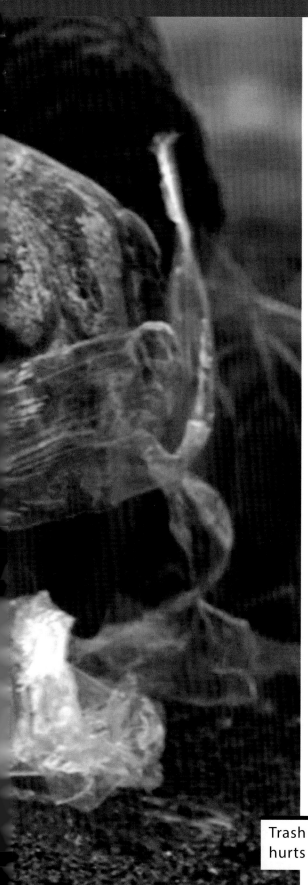

Trash in the ocean also creates trouble for turtles. Plastic bags and other trash are washed out to sea. Green sea turtles can mistake bags or balloons for jellyfish. The plastic gets stuck in the turtles' throats or stomachs. The turtles starve and die.

A disease also affects green sea turtles. It makes tumors grow on their bodies. Tumors are growths of skin. The growths are not normal. The tumors can make it hard for the turtles to eat, swim, and breathe. Sometimes the tumors cause green sea turtles to die.

Green sea turtles do not just face danger in the water. Turtles also face problems on land. Sea turtles need long stretches of quiet, dark beaches. Many people build homes and hotels along beaches. The sea turtles can no longer nest safely. The lights confuse baby turtles. They may crawl toward the lights. The lights are away from the ocean. The baby turtles never make it out to sea.

Trash in the ocean
hurts green sea turtles.

HELP FOR TURTLES

Many people work hard to make the world safer for green sea turtles. Many countries have laws to help green sea turtles. It is illegal to kill or catch green sea turtles or dig up their eggs. Some laws make people add special machines to fishing nets. These machines act like escape doors for turtles in the nets. They give the turtles a way to swim to safety.

People also work to clean up the oceans. They remove old fishing nets. They clean up trash on beaches and along rivers. This helps stop trash from ending up in the ocean.

The turtle's nesting beaches are also important. In some places, people try to stop houses and hotels from being built on natal beaches. Some seaside towns turn off their streetlights during hatching season. This helps the baby turtles find their way to the ocean. Some beaches are closed during hatching season. People even stand watch over the hatchlings. They make sure the turtles make it to the sea.

Scientists help, too. They study green sea turtles on their migration. They watch them in their feeding grounds using underwater cameras. They try to understand what green sea turtles eat, how they live, and what dangers they face. It is important to understand the green sea turtle. With help, these amazing creatures can continue to live and migrate in the world's oceans.

People must study green sea turtles to understand their migration.

QUIZ

1 What gives the green sea turtle its name?

A. The green fat under its shell

2 What has the most deadly sting in the world?

A. The box jellyfish

3 How long do green sea turtles usually live?

A. For 50 to 80 years

4 How fast do migrating green sea turtles swim?

A. 1 to 1.5 mph (1.5 to 2.3 km/h)

5 How do green turtles cut through tough sea grasses?

A. With ridges on their sharp beaks

6 Who came up with the name "Las Tortugas"?

A. Christopher Columbus

7 What guides the hatchlings to the ocean at night?

A. The light bouncing off the water

8 At what age are green sea turtles able to mate?

A. 20 to 50 years

9 How many turtles in each clutch will survive their first year?

A. Only one or two

10 How long are hatchlings?

A. 2 inches (5 cm)

KEY WORDS

carapace: A carapace is the upper shell of a turtle. A carapace helps keep a turtle's body safe from harm.

clutch: A clutch is a batch of eggs. A female green turtle lays a clutch in her nest.

cold-blooded: A cold-blooded animal's body temperature is warm or cool because of the temperature outside of its body. Because it is cold-blooded, the green turtle warms itself in the sun.

endangered: An animal is endangered when it is at risk of disappearing forever. The green sea turtle is an endangered animal.

habitat: A habitat is a place that has the food , water, and shelter an animal needs to survive. A green sea turtle moves from one habitat to another as it migrates.

hatch: To hatch is to break out of an egg. Baby turtles hatch from their eggs.

hatchlings: Hatchlings are baby turtles that have broken out of their eggs. Turtle hatchlings crawl on the beach to the sea.

natal beaches: Natal beaches are the places where sea turtles are born and later return to lay their eggs. Female green sea turtles lay their eggs on natal beaches.

plastron: A plastron is the bottom shell of a turtle. A turtle's plastron helps keep its body safe.

predators: Predators are animals that hunt and eat other animals. Tiger sharks are predators of green sea turtles.

reproductive: Reproductive is something related to having babies. Green sea turtles have a reproductive migration.

reptiles: Reptiles are cold-blooded animals that lay eggs to have babies. Turtles are reptiles.

INDEX

Log on to www.av2books.com

AV² by Weigl brings you media enhanced books that support active learning. Go to www.av2books.com, and enter the special code found on page 2 of this book. You will gain access to enriched and enhanced content that supplements and complements this book. Content includes video, audio, weblinks, quizzes, a slide show, and activities.

AV² Online Navigation

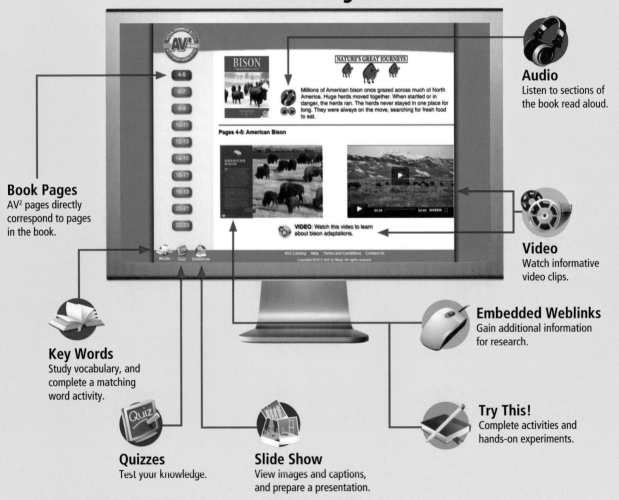

Audio
Listen to sections of the book read aloud.

Video
Watch informative video clips.

Book Pages
AV² pages directly correspond to pages in the book.

Embedded Weblinks
Gain additional information for research.

Key Words
Study vocabulary, and complete a matching word activity.

Try This!
Complete activities and hands-on experiments.

Quizzes
Test your knowledge.

Slide Show
View images and captions, and prepare a presentation.

AV² was built to bridge the gap between print and digital. We encourage you to tell us what you like and what you want to see in the future.

Sign up to be an AV² Ambassador at www.av2books.com/ambassador.